C'mon,
Let's hear it for Wales!
Cymru!

Jenny Sullivan

Illustrated by
Jac Jones

Pont

For Daisy Roo, Tove Bliss
and Catrin Fach
from Granny, and for
Kieran, Cassidy and
Izabel from Grannyjen
with all my love.

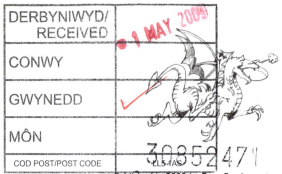

Published in 2009 by Pont Books, an imprint of
Gomer Press, Llandysul, Ceredigion, SA44 4JL

ISBN 978 1 84323 976 5
A CIP record for this title is available from the British Library.

© Copyright text: Jenny Sullivan, 2009
© Copyright illustrations: Jac Jones, 2009

Jenny Sullivan and Jac Jones assert their moral right under the
Copyright, Designs and Patents Act, 1988
to be identified respectively as author and illustrator of this work.

This book is published with the financial support of the
Welsh Books Council.

Printed and bound in Wales at
Gomer Press, Llandysul, Ceredigion

Contents

Playing for Wales

The Great Outdoors

On the Street

School Sports

Water, Water Everywhere

Hidden Talent

Playing for Wales

Millennium Stadium Haiku

Walk down Westgate Street,
Stadium soars proudly: white
Alien spaceship.

Cnapan

Once upon a time, I've heard,
In Wales there was a game,
The closest thing to rugby
And 'Cnapan' was its name.

They used a little ball of wood
Boiled to make it slippy,
And if you played at Cnapan,
You'd need to be quite nippy.

For hundreds, sometimes thousands
Would play on either side.
Most players ran around on foot
But gentlemen would ride.

Like rugby, there were line-outs
And many a scrum and maul:
They played all day for miles and miles,
Fighting to get the ball.

Cnapan isn't played today
And you might think that sad
But men were bashed and injured
And the chapels called it bad.

The players drank a lot of beer,
There weren't too many rules.
It's probably quite a lucky thing
It wasn't played in schools!

For if you play at rugby
You might just crack your head,
But if you played at Cnapan
You sometimes wound up – DEAD.

Old-timers

When Grandad and I walk past
that statue in Cardiff, right in the middle
of all the posh shops,
my grandad, he stands to attention,
sort of salutes and says,
'Now *that* was a player, that was!
Gareth Edwards. You won't see *his* like again.'

When we're watching rugby on telly
or sometimes down the Liberty Stadium
or Sardis Road, my dad says,
'Now *that* was a player! Scott Gibbs.
And those Quinnells. Ieuan Evans!
Those were the days.
We won't see *their* like again.'

But when it's a really special game:
Triple Crown, Championship, Grand Slam,
and I see Shane Williams skitter down the line
like a mad mosquito: dodging tackles,
sidestepping, jinking, accelerating, diving for a touch-
                                    down;
or James Hook pluck the ball from mid-air to score;
or Gavin Henson work his silver-booted magic,

I'm absolutely, positively certain
that no matter what my dad
and my grandad say
about Gareth Edwards, Ieuan Evans,
those Quinnells and Scott Gibbs,
we *will* see their like again –
because – we're Welsh, aren't we!

But It's a . . .

We're in the village rugby team
my mate Wil and me,
we train each Tuesday, rain or shine,
the best you'll ever see.

On practice nights from six till eight
we run and ruck and maul;
but Saturdays, I don't know why,
we don't do well at all.

We forward-pass and drop the ball
and though we're all quite tough,
it seems whenever we play a game
we haven't trained enough.

Last week, to make things even worse,
a stranger came to train.
I looked at Wil; he looked at me:
we moaned as if in pain.

'If we were bad before,' Wil said,
'we'll now be ten times poorer.
You don't imagine *She'll* turn out
to be our greatest scorer?'

The Girl said nothing, but she smiled
a secret kind of smile.
'Whatever!' said the coach. 'I think
we'll give the lass a trial.'

Game-time came on Saturday;
we trooped out on the field,
the Girl ran out behind us and
I knew our fate was sealed.

Although we're only under-tens,
we don't like getting smashed;
and with a girl at outside-half
we'd certainly get trashed.

But when the running started,
that Girl was off like lightning!
She spotted gaps and flicked the ball –
her speed was truly frightening.

She ran and dodged like Shane, she did.
The spectators started screaming.
We watched the scoreline mounting up
and hoped we weren't just dreaming.

We won! We won! We did high fives!
Best game we'd had all year.
We told the Girl we'd never seen
a player good as her.

'Of course you haven't,' said the Girl,
(first time we'd heard her speak).
'Just cross your fingers and your toes:
I *might* be back next week!'

The Touchline Dad

I'm in the school rugby team, and we play on Saturday mornings. It's great. We only play tag rugby but it's fast and fun, and us kids, we have a really great time, running and getting muddy.

But last Saturday we played this team from Cardiff, right? They came up in a big coach, so there was lots of room for mums and dads. They were all crowded on the touchline when the teams ran out. It felt fantastic, having spectators, although we're all only about ten (except Big Iwan – he's nine, but he's tall).

So. One of our dads was ref-ing, and we kicked off, and for a bit we had the ball. We were running with it – I passed it to Iwan – he passed it to Sioned – and then one of the dads (theirs, not ours) started shouting from the touchline.

'Don't let them have the ball! What's the matter with you? Can't you run? You're playing like a left-footed lummox!' he bellowed. 'You're hopeless!'

We knew whose dad it was, because one of the kids on the other side went bright red, the colour of a Welsh jersey ... and tripped ... and stumbled ... and dropped the ball.

His dad kept on: 'Good grief! Reff-errr-eee! Get yourself down the opticians, will you? That big kid was offside! That was a forward pass! You blind or what?'

The other mums and dads kept quiet. Didn't say a word.

Half-time, he stormed over to his kid and started waving his arms and shouting. The kid got redder. I think he was nearly crying. Then Betsan, our captain, gathered us in a team huddle. When we came out, we were all grinning.

Second half. Off we went. Big Iwan got the ball from me. We were heading for the line and sure enough that dad started up again: 'What's the matter with you, Ref? That was another forward pass!'

Then Betsan gave the signal and all of us, every one in our team, we stopped running. Stood *dead still* on the field. We folded our arms and glared at this kid's dad. Refused to run. Just stared. Glared.

And you know what? Next minute, so did the other team! And all the other mums and dads, and the touch judges, and the referee.

And the dad went redder than his kid. He went and sat by himself in their bus until the game was over.

We won, of course.

But, in a weird sort of way, so did the other team . . .

The Great Outdoors

Welsh Longbow

I take my arrow, straight and long,
Cock feather up, fit it to the bow,
Nock it, draw, strong wood resisting,
Pull back
And sight along the shaft.
The target blurs, I take a breath:
Steady. Draw. Exhale
And loose the shaft in one smooth
Movement,
Watch it fly true
And strike the gold.

I am connected, then,
By the pull of centuries, the link
Between this bright field
Of laughing people
Passing a summer's day
Sporting with arrows
To that time when
Archery was a nation's lifeblood.

They call it 'English longbow' now,
But once, it was pure Welsh.

Riding the Wind

They climb to the top of the hillside,
Strap a huge kite to their shoulders,
Leap into space and ride the wind
High over streams and boulders.
Sliding on waves of turbulent air,
Flying where the wind-tide flows,
Hovering above vast lakes of wheat,
Going where the wind-drift goes.
Sailing and soaring and drifting,
Sharing air with buzzard and kite,
Swooping and gracefully lifting,
Miraculous, magical flight.

I watch from my bedroom window
Bright specks in the crystalline sky.
I want to go where the wind-tides flow
Leap into the air – and fly.

Seasons

She comes when I call,
soft muzzle searching
for half an apple or
a fiery mint.
In spring, I saddle her
and ride emerald lanes
buttery with primrose,
starred with celandine,
through lapis bluebell pools.

In summer,
when biting flies madden her
we ride early, bareback
along the shore;
neat hooves splashing,
cantering at the edge
of the incoming tide,
before sandcastle crowds
flock like screaming gulls.

In autumn,
we ride the woods
flowing from summer
towards darkness and cold.
Leaves, gold and amber,

russet, some still showing
a last faint trace of green,
rustle underfoot.
She shies at rabbit-scuts.

On winter days, we ride
blue fields, where
early morning frost
crisps grass and hedges,
our breaths like dragonsmoke,
cobwebs limned in lace,
fragile air and brittle twig,
hooves striking iron on icy roads.

Saturdays Out with Dad

On Saturdays, if I haven't been
To my sister more than *normally* mean,
My dad will say, 'Well, come on, brat!'
And I know just what he means by that.

We get up early, dawn's first crack,
And put our bikes on the carrier rack,
Then we get in the car and drive away
And I know we'll have a fantastic day.

We drive to where the earth is mud,
Where the river roars in mighty flood
And mountain bikes go whizzing round
On tracks that twist along the ground.

We mount up, me and Dad, and bike
Up hills, down gulleys, where we like.
Mountain biking may be scary,
But as long as we are wary

We don't care about the weather,
When me and Dad are off together.
We tear about like maniacs,
Dad and me and biking tracks.

Castle Hill, Raglan

When we were little, if there was enough snow, the school closed because kids from the outlying farms couldn't get through the snow-full lanes. So then, all of us from the village had the day off too, and we'd dig out our sleighs from garages and attics (mind, some of us only had plastic feed-bags begged from farmers), and we'd go up Castle Hill, and slide down. Then we'd tow our sleighs all the way up and do it all again.

At the bottom, mind, you had to be careful. You had to know when to put on the brake or dig your heels in hard to stop because, at the foot of the hill, there was a stream ... But if it all went right and the sleigh runners found a streak of good snow we'd push off with our feet, my sisters and me, one behind the other and swoop down faster than a swallow in flight, wind blowing our hoods off, laughing into sharp blue skies.

We'd play for hours until it began to get dark and the sun slid pink on furrowed snow. Then we'd go home: wet gloves, soaked coats, cold feet, crimson cheeks and bruised knees, and Mum would fill us with hot soup, buttery toast, hugs and bedtime stories.

on the
street

But Where Can I Play, Gran?

My gran bought me a tennis racket
And a plastic tube of yellow balls.
Don't know why.
No tennis courts round here,
Not even a bit of a park.
I batted the ball up and down a bit.
Got bored.
I wanted to whack the ball *so hard*
The effort would make me grunt,
Have it fly back just as hard,
Whack it again with all my might.
But there's no courts round here
And, anyway, no one to play with.

And then
I found this *lovely wall* round the corner from our
house.
Red brick, with just one window high up in the eaves.
Fantastic!

I bounced the ball once, twice, three times,
Then smacked it, hard against red brick
(so hard I grunted).
The wall hammered it back like a Wimbledon finalist!
I bashed it again,

Thudded it back against the wall.
Thumped it,
Lobbed it,
Volleyed it,
Powered it.
Great!

But then a lady stuck her head
out of the window high in the eaves.
'If you don't stop hitting that ball . . .' she said . . .
'Don't make me come down there,' she said.
'I know where you live and I'll tell your mam.'

Honestly!
How will I ever get to Wimbledon
if no one will let me practise?

Stabilisers

My dad took the stabilisers off my bike.
'Come on,' he said, 'you can do it, I know you can!'
I wasn't so sure. I clutched the handlebars
really hard, and my spare fingers
hovered anxiously
above the brakes.
'I'll hold the saddle,' he said,
'so you won't fall.'
'Dad,' I said, a bit nervously,
'you won't let go, will you?'
'No,' he said.
'Promise?'
'Promise.'

So off we went, wobbly as a wonky wheel
at first, but then I got the hang of it.
Pedalled faster
and faster
and faster.
IcouldfeelthewindonmyteethbecauseIwasgrinning
SO HARD!
Dad was puffing along behind.
He was running really fast,
like a hare, or an Olympic sprinter.

'This is great, Dad!' I screamed into the wind.
He didn't answer. I looked down,
Saw my shadow,
MY shadow
not his . . .
And
So
I
Fell
Off . . .

Street Football

My grandad says
that when he was a little kid
him and his mates
used to play footie in the street.
They'd dump their coats on the mucky pavement
to make goalposts, sort of.
Then they'd spend the whole day
playing football. *In the street!*

Of course, that was in olden times
when no one had a car
and there weren't any lorries
thundering past
to get to the motorway,
'cos there wasn't a motorway back then
when my grandad played football in the street.

If me and my mates
did it now,
we'd probably get
walloped
for getting our clothes muddy,
shouted at
for bashing cars,
fined
for parking our coats,
or squashed
by a passing juggernaut.

And all for playing football in the street.

Can I Have a Skateboard
for Christmas Please?

I started round about July
To give them time to save.
'Can I have a skateboard please?
That's all I really crave.

'I'll be a sidewalk surfer,
The greatest ever seen,
And whizz along the pavement
And bend and jump and lean.'

I wanted one with the latest wheels
And a customised red deck,
But they wouldn't let me have it
Just in case I broke my neck.

'I can see it now,' my mam said.
'Off the path you'll rocket.
They'll only ever know it's you
By the contents of your pocket.'

So imagine my amazement
When beneath the Christmas tree
Was the strangest-looking parcel,
A skateboard just for me!

34

There were knee-pads and a helmet too,
And a box of skateboard tools,
But then they went and spoiled it,
With a set of stupid rules.

'No riding on the pavement.
No riding in the street.
You can skateboard in the garden
But keep off the garden seat!'

I looked out at the shrubbery,
I gazed at it for hours.
How could I learn to ride my board
Round lawns and trees and flowers?

And then I saw in the *Western Mail*
In print all bold and dark
'Great news for local youngsters
A NEW SKATEBOARDING PARK.'

I spend every minute down there,
Whizzing down the ramps,
Hurtling up the jump-offs
With all the other champs.

Oh there's nothing like a skateboard
For amazing, brilliant thrills
And sometimes (if I'm honest),
Some most spectacular spills!

Go-karting

My grandad told me that when he was small, he built this go-kart.

I said, 'Wow! That's fantastic! Where did you get the tyres and the engine, Grandad?'

Grandad laughed and said, 'Tyres? Engine? You've gotta be joking, boy! I had an old set of pram wheels and some planks of wood and a bit of rope. Engine? Tyres? Sissy stuff.'

'You what?' I said. 'Old wheels and wood? What use are they?'

So he showed me. He went down in the shed and got out my little sister's old pram. He unscrewed the wheels and the frame they were on, and he got some planks left over from building a wardrobe in the spare room.

And he built a go-kart.

Tell the truth, I was a bit dubious when he'd finished. It looked, like *really weird*. The front wheels swivelled and there was a rope to steer. And a bit of wood that you jammed down on the ground for a brake. Grandad towed me round the garden to show me how it worked. Dead boring. No engine to make it go. Then he went indoors to do his crossword. And I looked at this thing he'd built.

Next thing I knew, I was towing it down the garden path. Out the front gate, up the road to the top of the hill, Cwmdare Terrace stretching down to the main road at the bottom.

I got on the kart. Got hold of the steering rope, pointed downhill and kicked off. I went slowly at first, and then suddenly I was going fast. Very fast. Veryveryvery fast. I whizzed past Mrs Williams-Crosseyes on her doorstep and she waved her fist at me. I zoomed past Old Dai Bandy coming up the hill from his allotment and I rocketed past Jenny Flirty with her new boyfriend. So I waved. I like Jenny Flirty, but don't tell anyone.

Then, suddenly, I realised the main road was coming.

Fast.

I let go of the steering rope with my right hand and grabbed the brake. I hauled it on with all my might. It snapped off. I couldn't stop. What did I do? Well . . .

I shut my eyes and hoped I wasn't going to die. I heard some cars honk as the go-kart flew off the kerb. It took off like a jet fighter from an aircraft carrier!

It whooshed across the main road.

And crashed into the kerb on the other side.

Which is why
     I'm in hospital
          with concussion
               and my right leg
                    and my left arm
                         in plaster.
                              And it's also why
                    at the moment
               my mam and mam-gu
          aren't speaking
     to my grandad!

school

sports

Fairly Obstacular

'Right, you lot!' Mr Jones says
as we line up for Obstacle Race practice.
'You have to go under the netting; then
over the hoops,
one foot in each hoop without tripping;
along the benches without falling off;
pick up the hat and gloves and put them on.
Then you have to shift the chocolate finger
from one plate to the other,
using only the chopsticks provided;
knit a fancy sweater with
the needles and wool in the wastebasket;
swim fourteen lengths of a shark-infested pool,
carrying a house-brick in your teeth;
climb the fifteen-metre wall
without using your hands;
abseil down from the school roof
(after climbing up wearing frogman flippers and mask);
build a rocket and fire yourself to the moon,
fly back solo and then
wrestle a sabre-toothed hamster
single-handedly to the death;
train an elephant to cook sausage and chips;
clean a crocodile's teeth;
karate-chop the Headteacher
and race to the finish line.

That's all.
Ready?
One!
Two!
Three!
Go!

The Race

There's a little, chill wind
But though I'm wearing only
A vest and shorts, I don't feel it.

I feel only the smooth track
Under my running shoes,
The excitement of the race mounting.

We line up, six of us,
Shaking arm-muscles loose, flexing legs,
Stretching calves and ankles.

Down at the word, crouching,
Resting lightly on spread fingers,
Muscles tensed: ready.

A pistol cracks: we leave the blocks,
Seeing only bright lanes
ahead. Focused on the finish.

I stretch my legs,
Feel the hard track strike back,
Pump my arms and drive onward.

She's behind me. Gaining . . .
I accelerate – now I'm
Powering towards the finish.

I win: but all the ecstasy I feel
Is not in winning but purely
In the joy of running.

Emergency Sub

My junior school had a netball team.
Though I wasn't good enough
To play for the school in matches
And all that sporty stuff,

One day, while I was having tea,
A knock came at our door.
'A player's not turned up!' they said.
'We need you to make one more.'

'But I'm not a netball player,'
I protested. 'I'm too small!'
But they dragged me with them anyway:
'Even *you* can catch a ball!'

I'm afraid they were mistaken.
They should have listened better.
They hurried me into the yard
And stuffed me into a sweater.

It had some letters on it:
I'd no clue what they meant.
Someone blew on a whistle
And – hey-ho – off we went.

I stood there on the tarmac,
Daft as a chocolate hat,
Then everyone charged towards me
And knocked me down – KERSPLAT!

Well, that was much too shaming,
I jumped up and grabbed the ball,
Beat the other side's defenders,
Like they weren't there at all,

Raced to the tall goal-thingy,
The net up in the sky,
Then launched the netball upward
And watched it rocket high.

And miracles *can* happen:
The ball dropped through the net,
I waved my arms and jumped around:
I'd make the first team yet!

I was totally ecstatic,
Danced round the netball pole . . .
But then our captain yelled at me:
'You've just scored . . . an own goal!'

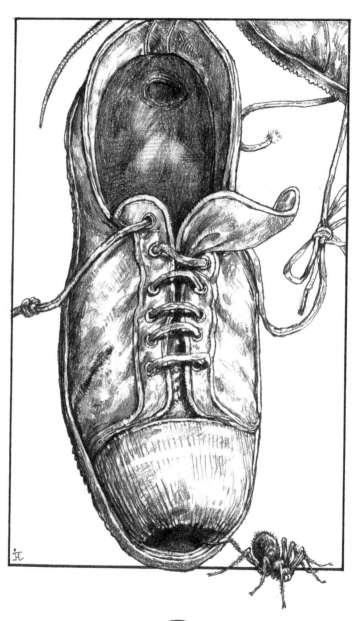

The Dap Box

When I was in primary school, we had to do PE in our knickers and vests. We didn't have timetables then, with *Arithmetic, English, Geography* and *Games* written out so we'd know when to bring our daps and stuff. And there wasn't a National Curriculum so you did games when Sir or Miss felt like doing it.

Some kids had posh cloth dap-bags with their names embroidered on them in chain stitch. My mam didn't have time for dap-bags and chain stitch – or even daps. There were such a lot of us in our house.

So, when Sir decided it was time for a games lesson, the dap monitors used to fetch the dap box from the games cupboard.

*

I hated that box. It was a big wooden crate full of daps. Black daps. Old daps. Smelly daps. Worn daps. Some were in pairs, tied together by their raggedy laces (no one had invented Velcro yet). Some didn't have laces at all. And they were *all too big*. Well, all the pairs I wore were. And I bet they were full of other people's verruca bugs! I'd have to put on these stinky daps with no laces, that were miles too big, so that I had to curl up my toes just to keep them on.

You try running with flappy shoes!

*

All the dap-bag kids with their chain-stitch names wore *their* daps, that fitted them. (George Pearson's were called 'plimsolls'. I liked George Pearson, except on dap-box days.) Us kids with busy mams – mams that weren't 'made of money' – slipped . . . and tripped . . . and wished . . .

Stuff I Can Do and Stuff I Can't . . .

If you were to ask me to run in a race,
Line up with the others in my place,
Wait for the starting pistol's crack
And pick up my feet and pound round a track,
Sorry, I honestly couldn't do that.

But . . .

Give me a pool that's clear and clean
Where the water's glistening turquoisey green,
Distorting the lines on the floor of the pool.
Well now, that would be really cool.
I could definitely do that.

But . . .

Ask me to do a Fosbury Flop
Or scream and do a karate chop
Or do a long jump or put a shot,
Sorry, those talents I haven't got.
I certainly couldn't do that.

But . . .

Dive in the pool and kick with my feet:
I'd be the winner of every heat.
I'd stay in my lane and I'd race down the length,
Fast as a porpoise with all of my strength.
I could brilliantly do that!

Then . . .

Turn underwater and push off the wall,
The end is in sight and I've beaten them all.
On the athletics field I'm a total fool
But I'll conquer the world in a swimming pool.
I really, definitely, honestly can

Do that!

High Board

Bare feet slap cold ridged tiles . . .
the ladder stretches up and up.
Are there clouds up there,
where the topmost board
stretches walk-the-plank
above the pool?
I climb. Hands clutch cold steel.
The diving board
shifts a little, as if
preparing itself
to take my weight.

I can do this.
Slowly to the very end.
The pool shimmers turquoise.
Turn. Face high windows.
Through frosted glass
ghost-cars stream.
Arms outstretched: step back,
toes gripped, heels in space.
Deep breath. Flex knees,
bounce once . . .
twice.
The board sings . . .
and then
I *fly* . . .
twisting,
tumbling,
falling
knifing
ice.
Bubbles stream past open eyes.

I'm grinning
underwater . . .
a perfect dive.

Dawn Surfer

The best times are dawn and sunset
when the rosy sky tints
the wings of swooping gulls
and the air is ice.
Wetsuit on – surf's up.
Paddle out, lifting into oncoming seas.
Outside, where the sea is calm,
I wait.
I know this coast, and how the waves
bow to harsh rocks,
curve into shore, and how they break
and curl.
I wait: just me, the wind
and the swelling sea.

And then, the wave.
The one
I've waited for. Drive the board
onto the crest and
ride it softly while it shapes
and peaks.
Skim down the glossy face,
emerald, crystal, overcurled. I am
surrounded,
sheltered by it, enclosed.

And then it releases me
and breaks: shatters into foam.

I paddle out to sea
to wait
where mighty waves are born.

Wild Water

When we were on holiday in north Wales last year, my dad took me canoeing. *Fantastic!* I thought. A nice peaceful afternoon paddling about on a quiet river, in the sun.

When we got to the canoeing centre, they made me put on a life vest even though I'm a really good swimmer and then they gave me a skidlid – which was when I got sort of suspicious.

I *heard* the river first: roaring and shouting like a rough schoolyard and then I saw it: hurtling and tumbling, crashing over jagged rocks. Water with an ASBO, it looked like! Serious, scary water. And this little, tiny canoe bobbing about on it. *Yeah, right,* I thought.

I said, 'Dad, you <u>want</u> me to go out there on that wild water, in that little eggshell thing?'

And Dad just grinned.

There was an instructor in the canoe as well as me. He gave me a paddle and said, 'Just do what I do, son. OK?'

'OK,' I said back and my voice sounded a bit shaky. I wondered if perhaps my dad was fed up with me . . .

Well. I can tell you that you can just forget about your fairground death drops and your thriller-spillers. This was the real thing! We didn't float; we hurtled. In and out of spiky rocks, tossed and tumbled on wild waters. We were up and then we crashed down. Spray drenched me, dripped off the end of my nose, got down inside my life vest and trickled icy down my chest. I collected some big blue bruises; grazed my elbow on a passing rock. I bit my tongue, once, and I could feel myself grinning.

I'm not sure whether it was a proper grin, or the scared-chimpanzee variety.

But at the end, when I got out on the bank
on my shaky, wobbly jellylegs,
I felt totally
abso-bloomin'-lutely
fabulous!

Hidden
Talent

Dreamers

Some people call football the Beautiful Game,
Wear the shirts of their favourite teams.
Millions of youngsters all over the land
Play football at night in their dreams.

They know that a scout for a famous club
Will lurk in the crowd with the aim
Of finding a boy who is good with a ball
And offer him fortune and fame.

And give him a one-in-a-billion chance
To be signed by a premier team,
To play for a side at the top of the League
And hear the supporters all scream:

'Come on, you reds!' (or you blues or you blacks!)
'You can win this game for us yet.
Sprint up the field like a bat out of hell.
Put the ball in the back of the net!'

And nobody knows, as they dream of a place
In the footballers' palace of fame,
Just which of those hopefuls will one day be great
And go right to the top of their game.

Kung Fu Barbie

My little sister's really small.
She looks like a doll, all frilly and curly,
If you saw my sister all dressed up
You'd think that she was really girlie.

But my sister's hobby is kung-fu fighting,
She goes twice a week to kung-fu class.
Don't mess about with my little sister
Or you'll end up landing on your . . .

. . . Um . . . Bottom!

Gymnast

When I started at the High School
I wasn't very tall,
And I wasn't good at team games:
I was really much too small.

I was hollered at in hockey,
In lacrosse I got lashed in the face,
I was utterly useless at rounders:
I could hardly get past first base.

But oh, when it came to gymnastics
There was no one better than me.
On the horse, the trampette and the wall bars
I was fast as a circus flea.

I'd bounce about on the baseboard,
I'd fly up the ropes like lightning,
Hang upside down from the top by my toes
And it wasn't the least bit frightening.

I could turn a cartwheel and stand on my hands,
Do back flips and star jumps and splits,
Head-over-heelses and stand on one leg:
I thrilled my teachers to bits.

They entered me in a gymnastic event,
I practised until I was shattered,
But then I came first and they gave me the prize
– well, none of the hard work mattered.

I may not be able to basket a ball
Or kick one into a net,
But gym is something I'm brilliant at:
There's a sport for you, too, I'll bet!